A Glittering Gallop

Conrad—the black and white nibbler

GROSSET & DUNLAP
Published by the Penguin Group
Penguin Group (USA) Inc., 375 Hudson Street, New York, New York 10014, USA

USA | Canada | UK | Ireland | Australia | New Zealand | India | South Africa | China
Penguin Books Ltd, Registered Offices: 80 Strand, London WC2R 0RL, England

For more information about the Penguin Group visit penguin.com

Text copyright © 2007 Sue Bentley. Illustrations copyright © 2007 Angela Swan. Cover illustration copyright © 2007 Andrew Farley. First printed in Great Britain in 2007 by Penguin Books Ltd. First published in the United States in 2013 by Grosset & Dunlap, a division of Penguin Young Readers Group, 345 Hudson Street, New York, New York 10014. GROSSET & DUNLAP is a trademark of Penguin Group (USA) Inc. Printed in the U.S.A.

Library of Congress Cataloging-in-Publication Data is available.

ISBN 978-0-448-46730-6   10 9 8 7 6 5 4

A Glittering Gallop

SUE BENTLEY

Illustrated by Angela Swan

Grosset & Dunlap
An Imprint of Penguin Group (USA) Inc.

Prologue

Lifting his head, the young white lion sniffed the hot breeze rustling through the thornbushes. It felt good to be home again. Maybe this time he would be able to stay.

Suddenly a terrifying roar split the air and an enormous adult lion appeared above him on a rocky ridge.

"Ebony!" Flame gasped, as he looked

up at the terrifying sight of his uncle.

He felt sparks igniting in his fur and there was a bright white flash. Where the majestic young white lion had been, there was now a tiny, fluffy calico kitten. Flame edged slowly back into the bushes, hoping that his white fur with ginger and black markings couldn't be seen.

Ebony's fierce eyes looked down, seeming to bore into Flame's tiny kitten body. Flame crouched low, trembling with anger and fear. There was a rustling sound behind him, and an old gray lion pushed through the bushes.

"Prince Flame. It is good to see you again. But you have returned at a dangerous time," Cirrus rumbled.

Flame blinked up at his old friend with relief. "I am glad to see you too,

Cirrus. I had hoped that my uncle would have given up looking for me."

"That will never happen," Cirrus told him sadly. "Ebony is determined to find and kill you, so that he can keep the throne he stole from you. You must go back to the other world and hide. Use this disguise well and stay safe."

"I am tired of hiding!" Flame mewed, his emerald eyes flashing. "I will face my uncle!"

Cirrus showed his worn teeth in a proud smile. "Bravely said, but first, you must grow strong and wise. Go . . ."

Suddenly another fierce roar rang out. Ebony charged down the rocks and came thundering toward the thorn bushes where Flame and Cirrus were hiding. The ground shook beneath his mighty paws.

"He's seen us! Go now, Flame!" Cirrus
urged. "Save yourself!"

The tiny kitten whined as he felt the
power building inside him. His fluffy
calico fur glittered with sparks, and there
was another bright flash. Flame felt himself
falling. Falling . . .

Chapter
ONE

Zoe Swann frowned as she looked up at her nana. "Do I have to?" she grumbled.

Joy Swann smiled, the sunlight glinting on her bright red hair. "Don't look so sad, sweetie. Anyone would think I'd asked you to fly to the moon, instead of collect a few eggs!"

Zoe looped the egg basket over

her arm. "Oh, all right," she said, making a face. "I guess I should do something, now that Mom's dumped me here!"

Her nana chuckled. "You know that your mom will write the book more quickly without interruptions. And then she can come down and stay for a few days, too."

"So I'm just an 'interruption'? Thanks a lot!" Zoe grumbled.

Joy ruffled her granddaughter's short blond hair. "Don't be so dramatic, Zoe!"

"Well, it's not my fault if Mom's silly old book won't behave itself, is it? I promised to creep around the house like a mouse in slippers, but she wouldn't listen," Zoe said bitterly. Her mom wrote children's books about a family who lived on a barge. They were really good but, to Zoe's annoyance, her mom couldn't have any distractions when writing them—including Zoe.

"It's not for long," her nana said, her smile wavering. "You know I love having you stay over, and I thought you liked staying with me."

"I do." Zoe felt an uncomfortable twinge of guilt. Her nana was great. She was funny and generous and not strict at all. But Zoe had planned to help out at the local stables over her vacation. After each morning mucking out, Lizzie, the stables' owner, let Zoe ride one of the ponies. Now she was going to miss out on all the riding opportunities.

"Off you go then," her nana said from
the back doorstep. "I'm going inside to
do some baking. Oh, by the way. I just got
a new bunch of bantams. Watch out for
Cocky. He can be a bit bad-tempered."

"I know how he feels!" Zoe muttered,
rolling her blue eyes.

Despite herself, she began swinging
her arms as she trudged down her

grandmother's endless garden. It
was hard to stay grumpy on such
a beautiful day. Bees flew back and
forth over the colorful flower beds.
There was a lovely smell of warm grass
cuttings and by the time she reached
the sturdy, wooden chicken house Zoe
had cheered up quite a bit.

She looked curiously at the
bantams. They were about half the size
of normal chickens. Some of them
had bright, glossy feathers and delicate
legs, and others were fat and fluffy and
looked like they were wearing baggy,
feathery trousers.

A handsome black cockerel ran out
toward the wire mesh of the outside
run that surrounded the chicken house.
His bright red crest was raised and

there was a fierce glint in his beady red eyes.

"Hi, Cocky," Zoe said.

The cockerel snapped his beak and flexed his strong clawed feet.

"Okay, I get the message!" Zoe backed away. She went around the chicken house and opened the nest box on the other side. "Wow! Look at these! I thought eggs were only white or brown!" The bantams' eggs were all shades of pale green, blue, and gray. There were even pink ones with little brown freckles.

Zoe filled the basket with eggs and then decided to take the long way back to the house, past the chickens and the greenhouse into the orchard.

As Zoe wandered toward the

greenhouse she noticed that the door was open. Inside she glimpsed a jungle-like mass of plants with tomatoes, peppers, and lots of stuff she didn't recognize.

Suddenly, from among all the plants, there was a flash of bright white light. "What was that?" A little nervously, she crept inside.

At first Zoe couldn't see anything odd as she walked between the rows of plants and flowers, but just as she was about to turn back, she noticed something glowing faintly at the very back of the greenhouse.

Zoe went forward slowly. As she got closer, she saw a big pile of old flowerpots in a corner, and on top of them there crouched what appeared to be a tiny kitten. In the light its fluffy coat seemed to sparkle all over. Zoe blinked hard. How did a kitten get in here?

When Zoe looked again, the sparkles seemed to have faded. The kitten was really cute, with white fur and ginger and black markings and the brightest emerald eyes Zoe had ever seen.

"What are you doing in Nana's greenhouse?" Zoe said aloud.

The kitten pricked up its tiny ears and looked straight at her. "I am hiding from my uncle, who wants to kill me," it mewed.

"Oh!" Zoe dropped the basket of eggs and her hands flew to her face in complete shock.

Chapter
TWO

Zoe stared at the calico-colored kitten in utter amazement. "Did . . . did you just speak?" she stammered.

The kitten nodded and lifted its tiny chin proudly. "Yes, I did. My name is Prince Flame, heir to the Lion Throne. What is yours?"

"I'm . . . Zoe. I'm staying here with my nana," Zoe answered, her mind whirling.

She couldn't believe this was
happening, but her curiosity was
beginning to get the better of her shock.
Bending down, she made herself seem
much smaller, so she didn't frighten the
little kitten away. "You're a prince? And
did you say that someone was trying to
kill you?"

"Yes. My uncle Ebony. He has stolen
my throne and rules in my place. One

day I will return and regain my throne," Flame mewed, his bright emerald eyes glittering with anger.

"But aren't you much too small to rule anyone?" Zoe asked gently. Flame said nothing, but his calico fur began to sparkle all over. He jumped off the flowerpots, and Zoe was blinded by a bright silver flash.

"Oh!" Zoe rubbed her eyes. When she looked again, she saw that the fluffy kitten had gone. In its place stood a magnificent young white lion.

Zoe gulped. Eyeing the huge paws and sharp teeth, she began to back away slowly.

"Do not be afraid. I will not harm you," the lion rumbled in a deep, velvety roar. There was another flash of light, and Flame reappeared as a tiny calico kitten.

"Wow! You really are a lion prince!" Zoe said, relieved and amazed at the same time.

"Yes. I am in disguise," the tiny kitten mewed, trembling from head to toe. "I must hide from my uncle's spies. Can you help me, Zoe?"

Zoe felt a second of doubt at the thought of Flame's evil uncle. But then she looked at the cute kitten. Flame was majestic as his real self, but in his kitten disguise he looked so helpless and frightened that her generous heart melted.

"Of course I will!" Zoe crooned. She bent down and picked Flame up. "I'll take care of you. Don't you worry about

your horrible old uncle. I bet he's no
match for my nana! Just wait until I tell
her about you!"

Flame squirmed. He reached up
a tiny white, ginger-tipped paw and
stroked Zoe's cheek. "You must tell no
one that I am a prince! It must be a
secret!"

Zoe frowned. She knew her nana
could be trusted.

"You must promise," Flame insisted. He blinked at her with wide, trusting eyes.

Zoe felt a bit guilty that she couldn't tell her nana, but if it would help keep Flame safe, she was prepared to agree. "Okay, I promise."

Flame rubbed the top of his fluffy head against her chin. "Thank you, Zoe."

"No problem. Let's go into the house. I imagine you're hungry," Zoe said.

Flame purred eagerly.

Zoe picked up the basket of eggs. Amazingly, none of them had broken. She held Flame close with her free hand as she went out of the greenhouse and headed toward the garden.

She could still hardly believe that she

had found a magic kitten. With Flame to take care of, it looked as if staying with Nana was going to be exciting after all!

"What an absolutely gorgeous kitten—and I love his name!" Zoe's nana said as soon as Zoe had introduced Flame. "Where did you find him?"

Zoe told her about finding Flame in the greenhouse.

Joy Swann frowned. "Strange. I wonder how he got into the garden. A tiny kitten like that couldn't have climbed the wall."

"Maybe he crawled under the back gate," Zoe suggested hurriedly. "Can I keep him, Nana? I promise I'll look after him. He can live in my room with me. If you let me keep him I'll feed the chickens, collect the eggs every day, and even be nice to the bantams!"

Her nana chuckled and gave Zoe's shoulder an affectionate squeeze. "I'm glad to see that you've cheered up at last. That long face you've been wearing since you arrived would have turned milk sour! Of course Flame can stay. But I'll let the local shelter know, and you'll have to be prepared for his owner to claim him."

Zoe nodded. "I will. Thanks a million, Nana." She didn't think anyone would claim this particular kitten!

While Nana made a quick phone call, Zoe took a can of sardines from the cupboard and forked them into a dish. "There you are, Flame."

Flame purred as he gobbled the sardines hungrily and then sat and licked his whiskers clean.

A few minutes later, Zoe's nana came back into the kitchen. "Now—about all those chores you've promised to do," she said with a twinkle in her eye.

"Yes?" Zoe said brightly, determined to show that she meant what she'd said.

"I was about to go and pick some raspberries . . ."

"Flame and I will do it." Zoe jumped up at once and took a plastic bowl from a shelf. "Come on, Flame!" she called.

Flame scampered outside after Zoe as she took a shortcut across the lawn to the orchard. The late afternoon sun cast long shadows from the apple trees. There was a summer house in one corner and a patch of fruit bushes nearby. Zoe began picking raspberries from their canes. "I love it down here. It's almost like a secret garden," she told Flame.

"It is warm and peaceful. I feel safe here," Flame purred happily, stretching out full length in the warm grass.

Suddenly Zoe saw a flash of reddish

brown and a slim shape dashed through the trees.

"Wow! A fox," she breathed.

She froze. But the fox had already seen her. It dashed toward the greenhouse and ducked under some bushes.

Flame sat bolt upright and gave an eager little mew.

"Did you see that fox, too? Wasn't it gorgeous?" Zoe said excitedly.

Flame didn't answer at first. He stared fixedly at a big, twisted tree that was near the garden wall. "There are some humans over there!"

"Where . . . ?" Zoe began, frowning.

A boy and a girl shot out from behind the tree and hurtled toward the garden wall. They both wore jeans, T-shirts, and sneakers and looked about ten years old, the same as Zoe.

"Hey!" Zoe yelled, sprinting after them. Those kids must have been trying to steal her nana's apples!

The kids reached the wall. They scrambled up the uneven stone, as agile as monkeys. The girl reached the top first. She swung her leg over and disappeared down the other side. When the boy got to the top, he crouched there on his knees and glanced over his shoulder.

Zoe caught a glimpse of a thin, worried face, glasses, and floppy dark hair.

Suddenly, the boy wobbled. He gave a yell. Almost in slow motion, he toppled backward.

"Oh no! He's falling!" Zoe gasped in horror.

Time seemed to stand still as Flame

appeared by Zoe's feet, sparks igniting in his fluffy calico fur and his whiskers crackling with electricity.

A warm tingle flowed down Zoe's spine and she shivered, strangely certain that something was about to happen.

Chapter
THREE

Flame lifted a tiny, ginger-tipped
white paw and a bright stream of sparks
shot out from it, hitting an empty bag
of candy at the base of the wall.

The bag instantly turned into an
enormous pile of giant, squishy pink
marshmallows.

It was only just in time.

"Oof!" The boy landed on the

massive marshmallow pile. His glasses
slipped off his nose and bounced on
to the grass as he sank deeper into the
pillowy marshmallows.

Zoe ran over to him. "Are you okay?"
she asked anxiously.

"I thought I was going to break a
leg!" the boy said, sitting up and looking
dazed.

"It would have served you right!"
Zoe said indignantly to this apple-
stealing boy, now that she could see he
wasn't hurt.

The boy blinked up at her
shortsightedly. "Who are you? What have
I landed on?"

Every time he moved, he slid and
bounced about on the marshmallows.
Pink blobs were stuck all over his hair
and face. He looked so funny that Zoe
had to bite back a smile.

"Um . . . leaves and grass and stuff!"
she improvised, making frantic waving
signs to Flame behind her back.

Flame waved his paw again. To Zoe's
relief, the pile of marshmallows magically
transformed into a big pile of apple-tree
leaves. She saw that every bit of pink

marshmallow had disappeared from the
boy and the sparkles had faded from
Flame's fur.

The boy pushed himself on to his
knees and started feeling all around
him. "Where are my glasses? I can't see
a thing without them."

"Well done, Flame," Zoe whispered,
as she started looking for the glasses.

Flame purred and rubbed himself
against her ankles.

Zoe spotted the glasses in a patch
of long grass. Picking them up, she
handed them to the boy. "Here you
are."

"Thanks." The boy put his glasses
on and pushed his floppy dark hair out
of his eyes. "Hi! I'm Todd Trapman," he
said, flashing Zoe a grin. "I live next

door. What are you doing here? I haven't seen you before."

"I'm Zoe. I'm staying with my nana. This is her garden, and you're trespassing!" Zoe said. "I should report you for stealing her apples!"

"Me and Todd weren't stealing!" called a girl's voice.

Zoe looked up to see a girl perched on top of the wall. She had floppy, dark hair, too, but hers was long and tied into a ponytail. Except for the glasses, she looked exactly like Todd.

"That's my sister, Tracy," said Todd.

"You're twins," Zoe said.

"Ten out of ten for observation!" Tracy joked.

Zoe couldn't help grinning. "Well, anyway, what were you doing in here?"

The twins exchanged wary glances. "Don't tell her, Todd. I don't think . . ." Tracy began.

"It's okay, Tracy. She helped me just now. I think we can trust her," Todd said.

"We've been coming over here to feed Bracken. We think she's probably had cubs," he explained.

"Bracken?" Zoe asked, confused.

"The fox that lives near here," Tracy explained.

Zoe's face lit up. "Oh! I just saw her!"

Todd nodded. "She knows us now, but she's still shy around strangers. That's why she ran away when she saw you."

"She hasn't brought her cubs here yet, but we're sure that she will when she thinks it's safe. We're dying to see them," Tracy added.

Zoe felt excited. It would be great to
see Bracken with her cubs.

"That's a really cute kitten. Is it
yours?" Todd said suddenly, bending
down to stroke Flame's tiny ears. The
calico kitten purred in appreciation.

Zoe nodded. "Yes. His name is
Flame. I, um . . . haven't had him long."
She looked up at Tracy. "Why do you
and Todd come over the wall? It's really

dangerous. I bet my nana would let you use the gate if you asked her."

"As if!" Tracy scoffed. "People who have chickens aren't very eager to take care of foxes. She's more likely to want to poison Bracken."

"She wouldn't!" Zoe cried, horrified. "Nana loves wildlife. She won't even use slug pellets, in case a hedgehog eats one."

"Really?" Todd said. "Maybe we *could* ask her, Tracy."

Tracy's eyes blazed. "No way! You swore we'd keep it a secret! Bracken relies on us, and I'm not letting her down. We can't risk it."

"But think about it, Tracy. I nearly broke my leg falling off the wall today. It would be a lot easier to come in through the garden gate," Todd said reasonably. "What about if Zoe puts in a word for us with her nana? Would you, Zoe?"

Zoe thought about it. She decided it would actually be nice to have some people her own age around. "Okay. We can go and ask her now if you like."

"Ask me what?" said a voice behind Zoe.

Joy Swann came through the trees. "I came to see why you were taking so long to pick those raspberries." She looked at Zoe and Todd, who was still stroking Flame. "Who's your young friend, Zoe?" she asked and then she glanced up at Tracy. "And would someone like to tell me why there's a girl sitting on the top of my garden wall?"

Chapter
FOUR

". . . and that's why Todd and Tracy
have been climbing into the orchard
for the past few weeks," Zoe finished
explaining about Bracken.

Her nana nodded, taking it all in,
and then she smiled. "Well, I must say
it's nice to meet my new neighbors at
last—even if it is in a rather unusual way!
I was wondering who'd moved into the

old barn buildings across the back field."

Todd smiled with relief, but Tracy still looked a little worried. "You . . . you won't tell our parents about this, will you?" she asked. "Dad will go crazy if he finds out!"

"As you're not going to be climbing over my wall from now on, I don't think I need to speak to your parents," Zoe's nana said. "Now, why don't we all go into the house, and you can have something to eat while you tell me a bit more about Bracken."

In the kitchen, Zoe and the twins sat at the kitchen table. Zoe stroked Flame, who was curled up on her lap.

Her nana fetched cool drinks and then passed around a plate piled with warm muffins, topped with butter and raspberries.

"Wow! Thanks, Mrs. Swann," Todd said, digging in.

"Call me Joy," she replied, smiling and listening with interest as the twins told her their suspicions that Bracken had had cubs.

"We've seen her near the gardens at the back of Bants Lane a couple of times. We think she has a den over there," Tracy told her.

Joy Swann nodded. "That's a likely place for a fox's den. Some of those gardens are really overgrown. Let me know if Bracken brings her cubs into my garden. I'd love to see them."

"We will!" chorused Todd and Tracy.

"The old summer house is a good spot for a night watch, if you'd like to come over sometime!" Zoe's nana said with a twinkle in her eye.

"Cool!" Todd said.

Tracy's eyes widened in surprise. "How come you don't mind having a fox coming into your garden? What about your chickens?"

Joy Swann pushed a strand of unruly bright red hair off her face. "I built the henhouse myself. The run's fox-proof, and I always shut the bantams away at night for good measure. Unless Bracken brings a pair of wire-cutters with her, my chickens are pretty safe!"

Everyone laughed.

"Thanks very much for the muffins, Mrs. Swann—I mean, Joy," Todd corrected himself. "We have to go now. Our ponies need exercising."

Zoe was giving Flame a blob of cream on her finger. Her head popped up. "Ponies?"

Tracy nodded. "We've got three: Fudge, Patch, and Ginger. They're gorgeous. Why don't you come over tomorrow and meet them?"

"I'd love to. I'll bring Flame, too. Can I, Nana?" Zoe asked eagerly.

"'Course you can, sweetie," her nana said. "I've got some shopping to do anyway, and I imagine you're not interested in coming with me."

Zoe grinned. "Ponies or shopping? Sorry, Nana. It's no contest!"

The following morning, Zoe woke up with a strange noise in her ear. It took her a few moments before she realized that it was Flame purring beside her on the pillow.

"Hello, you," she crooned, tickling him gently under his chin. "Did you sleep well?"

"Very well, thank you," Flame purred more loudly.

"We'd better get up. We're going over to Todd and Tracy's, remember?" Zoe threw back the covers and quickly got dressed.

Downstairs, she fed Flame first and then ate breakfast with her nana. She was in such a good mood that she put the breakfast dishes in the dishwasher without being asked.

Her nana looked pleasantly surprised. "Thanks, Zoe. Are you ready? I'll walk along the lane with you to Todd and Tracy's. It's on the way to the stores, and I thought I'd bring them a few raspberries."

Zoe and Flame followed her outside the front door and they turned immediately left into Bants Lane. Flame scampered along beside Zoe. He nosed about in the long grass, eagerly sniffing all the country smells.

"He's very confident for such a tiny kitten," Zoe's nana commented.

"Yes, he is." Zoe smiled, wishing that she could tell her that Flame was really a young white lion!

After a couple of minutes they came to a large, fenced field, which followed the curve in the lane. As the path straightened out, Zoe saw the old barn and the long pebbled drive leading up to it.

"The Trapmans have made a good
job of those tumbledown old buildings,"
Zoe's nana said, looking at the sparkling
honey-colored stone walls and new roof.

The front door was opened by a slim
woman with dark hair, wearing jeans
and a pink blouse. "Hello, you must be
Joy Swann and Zoe. Tracy and Todd told
me you had them over yesterday. That
was very kind of you. Come in," she said
with a warm smile.

"Hello, Mrs. Trapman," Zoe said
politely.

As Zoe, her nana, and Flame went
into the kitchen, Todd appeared at
the back door wearing jeans tucked
into rain boots. "Hiya, Zoe!" he said,
beaming. "Come with me. Tracy's in the
stables."

With Flame at her heels, Zoe followed Todd.

"Have a lovely morning with Todd and Tracy. I'll see you later," her nana called after her.

"What lovely raspberries. Thank you. Do you have time for a cup of coffee?" Mrs. Trapman asked Joy.

Todd grinned at Zoe. "Your nana and my mom seem to be getting along well."

Zoe nodded. She saw Tracy coming out of the stables wheeling a barrow full of soiled straw and droppings.

Tracy looked up and smiled. "Hi! I won't be a minute. I'm just going to dump this."

"Can I help?" Zoe offered.

Tracy looked pleased. "Thanks. You can put down some fresh straw if you like.

Todd will show you where things are."

Todd led the way into the stables. Zoe picked Flame up and followed him. She couldn't wait to meet the ponies. There were six stalls in the stables. Three were empty, but there was a pony in each of the remaining stalls.

"This is Patch," Todd told Zoe, stroking the first pony's nose.

Zoe saw that Patch was a handsome light bay with a white blaze. Next Todd showed her Ginger, who was also a light bay with four white socks. "And this is dear old Fudge," Todd said, pointing to a light brown pony with a pale mane and tail.

"Hello, girl," Zoe said softly, patting the palomino pony's shoulder. Fudge put her ears forward and whickered a soft greeting.

Out of the corner of her eye, Zoe saw Flame pounce on a wisp of straw. He growled and started play-fighting. "Don't go too near the ponies' hooves, in case they kick out," she warned him.

Flame immediately sat down. Looking up at Zoe with bright emerald eyes, he pricked his ears. Fudge swung her head

down toward the tiny kitten and gave a
friendly snort.

"Sounds like that kitten understands
every word you say," Tracy said, coming
back into the stables. "And look at old
Fudge. She's really taken by him!"

Zoe smiled secretly to herself. She
helped Todd and Tracy put down fresh
straw, fill water buckets, and refill hay
nets.

Flame found a sunny corner and
curled up in the clean hay for a snooze.

"Shall we tack up and take the
ponies out now? Do you want to ride
Fudge, Zoe?" Tracy said.

"I'd love to!" Zoe exclaimed. She
had been hoping the twins would
suggest that she ride the palomino
pony! Then she remembered something.

"Oh, I didn't bring any riding gear to my nana's."

"What size shoes do you wear?" asked Tracy. Luckily, Zoe and Tracy wore the same size. Tracy loaned her a pair of jodhpur boots, a hat, and some gloves.

Tracy ran into the house to tell her mom where they were going. When she returned, they all mounted. Zoe rode along behind Todd on Patch and Tracy on Ginger. She patted Fudge's smooth, warm neck.

It felt wonderful to be riding again. It was her favorite thing in the whole world. Suddenly she felt her heart miss a beat. Flame! In all the excitement, she had left him behind at the stables!

Chapter
FIVE

Zoe felt terrible. She had to go back for Flame, right now. She was supposed to be keeping him safe!

Just as she was about to turn Fudge around, she spotted a familiar little calico-colored shape beside the track.

"Flame!"

The tiny kitten was running fast, his paws skimming the ground and his tiny tail stretched right out behind him.

Zoe stopped Fudge. Ahead of her, Todd and Tracy carried on, unaware that she had fallen back.

Flame's fur sparkled as he launched himself straight up into Zoe's arms.

"I am sorry, Zoe!" he panted, purring loudly. "I only just woke up and realized that you had gone. You like horses very much, don't you?"

Zoe stroked his soft little ears, still feeling guilty. "Yes, I do. But that's no excuse for leaving you behind," she whispered. "I'm really sorry."

"I am here now," Flame mewed, settling into her lap as she squeezed her legs against Fudge, urging her on.

Todd was waiting on Patch for Zoe for catch up. "Anything wrong?" he asked as Zoe rode up to him.

Zoe shook her head. "Not anymore," she murmured.

Flame was perfectly happy, looking all around with alert eyes as they rode along. He didn't seem to mind that she had forgotten him, but Zoe still couldn't forgive herself.

Todd urged Patch on. "We're turning on to a wider track up ahead.

It leads to Hackleton Firs."

No one else was around, so Todd, Tracy, and Zoe urged their ponies into a trot. Zoe drew level with Todd and rode beside him, while Tracy entered the large area of fir trees ahead of them.

The sun was warm on Zoe's bare arms. It was quiet except for the sound of the ponies' hooves. Tall fir trees stretched overhead and the bridle paths wove through thick bracken.

Zoe saw an older boy on a dark-bay thoroughbred pony coming toward them through the trees. The boy noticed Tracy on Ginger, but instead of slowing down as she would have expected, he urged his pony into a canter.

"What's that rider doing?" Zoe said, puzzled.

"Hey!" Tracy shouted, as the boy on the bigger pony rode so close to her that Ginger laid his ears back and shied to one side.

The older boy ignored her. "You kids! Get out of my way!" he shouted at Todd and Zoe, as his pony thundered toward them.

Todd and Zoe had stopped their
ponies. Todd just managed to pull Patch to
one side of the track. Zoe tried to move
aside, too, but Fudge snorted and pulled at
her bit in alarm.

The older boy pulled on the reins and
only just managed to avoid jostling Fudge.
"Why didn't you move, you stupid kid?"
he shouted.

As Zoe looked up into his mean eyes
and set face, her temper rose. "You could
have slowed down. You had plenty of
time!" she shouted back.

"You little . . ." The boy's face
darkened. He flapped his arms at Fudge.
"Go on! Ya-ah!"

Fudge rolled her eyes in fright. She
leaped forward, crashing through the tall
ferns that lined the track.

Flame yowled fearfully. He dug in his claws and hung on to the saddle.

Zoe pulled at the reins, but Fudge was terrified by the bracken stems lashing against her legs and belly. Suddenly a low thorny hedge appeared in front of her. Zoe's heart rose into her mouth. Fudge didn't slow down. She was going to crash into it!

Sparks ignited in Flame's calico fur, and his whiskers crackled with electricity. A tingling sensation prickled down Zoe's back.

Flame raised a tiny paw and a snowstorm of glitter whirled around Zoe and Fudge.

Three strides, two strides, one stride . . .

Zoe flinched and then gasped as Fudge soared high into the air on a curving bridge of silvery glitter. The pony cleared the hedge easily and landed safely on the bridleway on the other side. Fudge came to a stumbling halt and stood there, trembling.

"Thanks, Flame! You were amazing!" Zoe said shakily, giving him a hug before stroking Fudge's neck to calm the old pony down.

"You are welcome," Flame purred. Sparks still twinkled in his fluffy fur as he leaped down onto the track like a tiny comet.

Zoe smiled at him, even more determined now to look after this incredible magic kitten and keep him safe.

"Zoe! Are you all right?" shouted Tracy, interrupting her thoughts as she rode toward her. Todd was just behind his twin.

Zoe quickly glanced at Flame, but the sparks had all faded from his fur.

"We saw Fudge bolt and cut across to head you off!" Todd called.

"I'm fine, and Fudge's okay, too," Zoe said. "She . . . um, jumped the hedge."

Todd and Tracy looked at each other in amazement. "Old Fudge jumped that hedge?"

Zoe nodded. *With a bit of help from Flame!* she thought gratefully. "That horrible boy deliberately startled her. It's lucky Fudge wasn't badly hurt."

"That was Jake Fawsley. He's a real pain," Tracy said.

"Does he live around here?" Zoe asked.

Todd nodded. "His dad's Master of the Hounds for the local race. He's a really nice man, but Jake's full of himself and thinks he can do just what he likes!"

Zoe remembered the glimpse of the older boy's mean face. "How about we continue with our ride? I don't see why that rotten bully should spoil it for us!"

"Definitely!" Zoe and Todd agreed.

Zoe bent down and lifted Flame carefully up onto Fudge's back and then remounted. Flame purred contentedly in Zoe's lap as she and the twins rode along the bridleways and eventually emerged back out onto the fields.

Chapter
SIX

When they got back Todd, Tracy, and
Zoe untacked the ponies and turned
them out into their paddock. Then Zoe
and Flame went back to her nana's for
lunch.

"Did you have a good time with
the twins?" Joy Swann asked her
granddaughter.

"Yes, we went riding in the Firs. I

think Flame really enjoyed it, too," Zoe said.

She didn't mention Jake Fawsley or Fudge bolting, as she had a sneaking feeling that if she did she might not be allowed to go riding again.

"Can I open a can of tuna for Flame, Nana?" Zoe asked. *He deserves a special treat after the way he saved Fudge and me*, she thought.

After lunch, Zoe did a couple boring chores for her nana, and then spent a few hours in the garden with Flame. She dragged a twig around for him to chase for a while, and then he stretched out beside her while she read a magazine.

It was just starting to get dark when the twins arrived with some food for Bracken. Zoe and Flame went down to

the orchard with them and helped scatter
the food within sight of the old summer
house. Zoe felt a flicker of excitement
as she prepared for her first evening fox-
watching with the twins.

They all made themselves
comfortable and then sat looking out
into the gathering dusk.

"How do you like fox-watching so
far?" Zoe whispered after a few minutes
to Flame as he curled up beside her on
the warm floorboards.

"I like it very much," he mewed
softly.

Todd and Tracy sprawled on their
stomachs side by side, peering at the
orchard through the open doorway. "I
wonder if Bracken will bring her cubs
tonight," Todd said.

"Oh, I hope so," Zoe said eagerly.

After about half an hour, when Bracken still hadn't arrived, Todd sat up and pushed back his floppy, dark hair. "Tracy and I had a great idea earlier," he told Zoe. "We have something to ask you."

"You do?" Zoe said, intrigued.

"Yes. We're riding in a competition at the town fair next weekend. We wondered if you'd like to be in it with us," Todd said.

"You could ride Fudge," Tracy added. "That jump yesterday was really impressive! I don't know how you got her to do it. She's such a sweet, lazy old thing."

"I'm not sure I could do it again," Zoe said, biting back a smile. She wished she could tell them how Flame had saved them by getting Fudge over the hedge himself, but a promise was a promise. "I'd love to ride in the competition!"

"Great!" chorused the twins.

Zoe laughed.

"If you come over tomorrow," said Todd, "you can help us put up a jumping course in the field. We can practice together every day until the show."

Zoe grinned. "Awesome! Did you hear that, Flame?"

Flame gave an eager little mew.

Tracy chuckled. "He just answered you!"

"Shhh! I just saw something over by the greenhouse," Todd whispered.

Zoe watched closely as a slim red shape emerged from a bush near the greenhouse and began weaving toward them through the shadowy trees. "It's Bracken!"

Her eyes widened. She had never been so close to a real, live fox. Bracken was smaller than she remembered, with a delicate muzzle and a black tip to her tail. She had slender limbs and moved more like a cat than a dog.

Bracken went straight to the food spread out on the grass and began eating hungrily.

"Still no sign of any cubs," Tracy whispered disappointedly.

"At least we can keep watch," Todd whispered back. "When she does bring them, we'll be waiting."

By the time Bracken had finished eating, the moon had risen, making the

grass look silver and casting the trees
into pools of deeper shadow. The fox
slipped away as silently as she had
arrived.

Tracy and Todd stood up and
stretched. Zoe and Flame walked down
to the garden gate with them.

"See you tomorrow," the twins called
as they went out into the lane.

"You bet," Zoe said, waving. She
was looking forward to putting up the
jumps and riding Fudge again. "Come
on, Flame. Let's go in and tell Nana that
we've seen Bracken."

Bright and early the next day, Zoe
and Flame walked up Bants Lane to the
Old Barn. Todd and Tracy were already
in the field, setting up jumps.

Zoe helped with the jumps. She couldn't believe how well her vacation was turning out—not only was she able to do some riding after all, but she had Flame with her, too: her own magic kitten!

At last, after mucking out and grooming, the ponies were saddled up. Flame climbed up a fence post and settled down to watch.

Todd and Tracy were experienced jumpers. Their ponies, Patch and Ginger, even seemed to enjoy going over the low jumps. Zoe felt her stomach clench with nerves when it was her turn. She hadn't done much jumping, and Flame couldn't use his magic to help her with the twins watching.

She pointed Fudge toward the first

jump. What if Fudge was nervous after
her fright in the Firs yesterday? Fudge
eyed the jump. She started to slow down.

Zoe clicked her tongue. "Come on,
girl!" she said firmly, pressing her on.

Fudge tossed her head. She sped up
again and suddenly they flew over the
jump.

"Hurrah!" yelled the twins. "Well done, Zoe!"

Zoe beamed at them. After that, Fudge seemed to get her confidence. She went over all the jumps perfectly. As she trotted back past the fence where Flame was crouched watching, Fudge twitched her ears and gave a friendly neigh.

Flame sat upright and meowed loudly.

"Look at that. They're saying hello to each other!" Todd said, laughing.

Zoe smiled to herself. The kitten and pony had become good friends. She suspected that Fudge somehow knew that Flame had saved her from getting hurt when she had bolted up at the Firs.

Over the next few days, Zoe
and Flame spent a lot of time at the
Trapmans' house. With all the practice,
Zoe gained confidence, and Fudge was
now responding to her really well. She
couldn't wait to be in the competition.

One evening, Todd, Tracy, Zoe, and
Flame were all on fox-watch in Nana's
summer house as usual. They had seen
Bracken incredibly close almost every
evening, but still hadn't spotted any sign
of her cubs.

Zoe watched Bracken appear from
behind the bush near the greenhouse.
She noticed that the vixen seemed very
wary. Instead of eating the food right
away, she sniffed it and then lifted her
head and looked around.

"She's acting a bit strange," Zoe whispered.

"Zoe's right. Why isn't Bracken eating the food?" Tracy said.

Bracken lifted her delicate muzzle and sniffed the air. She gave a low cry.

Todd frowned and pushed his glasses on to the bridge of his nose. "That's strange. She seems to be calling to someone. You know what I think . . . ?"

"Yes!" Tracy and Zoe leaned forward eagerly, with shining eyes.

Two small red shapes came out of the bush. The cubs were about half the size of their mother, with thick bushy tails. They crept forward hesitantly and trotted through the orchard. When they reached the food, they began eating, watched over by Bracken.

"Oh, aren't they gorgeous!" Zoe
whispered in awe.

She and Flame, and the twins, watched
as the cubs finished eating and then played
a game of tag. Bracken stood by as they
rolled around play-growling. Even when
she led the way out of the garden the cubs
ran along after her, trying to bite her tail.

Todd, Tracy, and Zoe fell over
laughing. "The little rascals!"

Later, after telling her nana all about the wonderful cubs, Zoe went up to her room. She opened the window and leaned out on to the moonlit garden.

"Clever Bracken! Two healthy cubs," she said, yawning. "I wonder if her den is on the garden. Maybe we could all ride over and have a look sometime. What do you think, Flame?" she asked sleepily.

There was no answer.

Zoe turned back into the room to where Flame's tiny form was curled up on her bed. His whiskers twitched and his tiny paws flexed as he slept. Was he dreaming of his own world and the Lion Throne, which he would one day claim?

She felt a surge of affection for him. She hoped it would be a very long time before he had to leave.

Chapter
SEVEN

Zoe narrowly avoided the cockerel's sharp beak as she tipped out the last of the corn. Stepping outside the chicken run, she shut the door tightly.

"That Cocky's a nightmare," she said to Flame. "It's a good thing that you stayed outside the run."

Flame gave Cocky a wary glance

before following Zoe to the feed shed. The cockerel was almost twice his current size.

"Okay. Chores finished. I'll just go and tell Nana that we're going over to see the twins." A gust of cool wind ruffled Zoe's short hair as she closed the door of the shed, and zipped up her jacket.

"I like riding with you, Zoe," Flame purred.

Zoe picked him up and gave him a cuddle. "You like old Fudge, don't you? She's fond of you, too."

When Zoe and Flame got to the Old Barn, Todd and Tracy already had the ponies saddled up. "We thought we'd go out for a ride instead of practicing jumping this morning," Tracy said.

"Fine by me," Zoe said, lifting Flame
up on to Fudge, before mounting. "Can
we go past the gardens? I was thinking
we might see Bracken."

"Good idea," Todd said.

They rode down the drive and
carefully crossed Bants Lane. After
passing a row of houses, they turned
onto a track that led along the side of
the gardens.

Flame was snuggled inside Zoe's jacket, with just his head poking out. As she rode, Zoe glanced toward a tangled hedge of hawthorn. There was a flash of red as a fox darted into the bottom of the hedge.

Zoe stiffened. "Look! Over there!"

Todd and Tracy had seen Bracken, too.

"You were right about her den. It must be somewhere near that hedgerow," Todd said. "We'd better not go any closer, or we might scare the cubs."

They continued riding along the track, which opened out onto some fields. After about an hour, they turned back and retraced their steps.

As they came back toward the gardens, Zoe was riding alongside Tracy. She heard the barking of hounds.

"That's Mr. Fawsley exercising the pack. I bet Jake's with him," Tracy said. She didn't look very pleased at the idea of seeing the unpleasant boy again.

Zoe didn't want to meet him again, either. She still felt angry at the way Jake had deliberately startled Fudge.

The barking was getting louder. Zoe felt a flicker of alarm. The hounds were coming this way! "What about Bracken and her cubs?" she cried.

"If they get the scent of a fox, he'll never be able to call them off," Todd said.

"We have to ask Mr. Fawsley to take the hounds somewhere else!" Zoe said urgently, pressing Fudge into a trot.

Plunging forward, she sped down the track. As she rounded a bend, she came upon the pack of milling hounds cutting across a field toward her. She pulled on Fudge's reins and the pony slowed to a halt.

"There's a fox and her cubs in the gardens. Can you turn the hounds around, please, Mr. Fawsley?" she called breathlessly to a tall dark man in a tweed jacket.

Mr. Fawsley was surrounded by the pack of big, handsome hounds, all wearing wide doggy grins and wagging their tails. There was a boy with him. Zoe recognized him. It was Jake.

Mr. Fawsley looked up at Zoe and gave a friendly smile. "Hello, there! What's that about a fox?"

"Leave it to me, Dad. I met this kid the other day," Jake said curtly, striding up to Zoe.

"Yes, at Hackleton Firs, when you nearly ran me over!" Zoe flashed at him. "Fudge bolted because of you. We could both have been badly hurt!"

"Is this true, Jake?" his father asked sternly.

Jake swallowed. "'Course not. What do you take me for?"

Zoe gaped at Jake, shocked by the blatant lie, but there wasn't time to argue. "Please can you turn back the hounds, Mr. Fawsley? Bracken, a fox we know, has a den with cubs in the gardens."

"Oh, sure. Thanks for . . ."

Before his father could finish speaking, Jake roughly grabbed Fudge's bridle. "Tough! We've got a right to cut through the gardens if we feel like it!" he sneered at Zoe.

"Jake! There's no need for that!" said Mr. Fawsley.

Jake ignored his father and tugged at Fudge's bridle. The pony laid her ears back and took a step backward.

Zoe heard an indignant meow from inside her jacket, as sparks lit up in Flame's fur and his whiskers glowed with power. Zoe felt the familiar tingling down her spine. *Now you've done it, Jake Fawsley*, she thought.

Jake's eyes widened in surprise. "Ye-ow! That's hot!" he yelled, jerking his hand back from Fudge's bridle. Suddenly, he flew backward as if he had been shot out of a cannon, and sat down hard on his bottom.

"Well done, Flame!" Zoe whispered.

By now Todd and Tracy had caught up. When they saw Jake sitting on the ground, they both started laughing.

Jake snarled, rubbing his sore hand. His face was as red as a beet as he got up. "I'll get you for that . . ."

Mr. Fawsley strode forward, grabbed his son by the collar, and heaved him to his feet. "That's enough, Jake! Help me with the hounds!" he ordered. "And I'll have something to say to you later!" He looked at Zoe. "I apologize for my son. Don't worry. I'll deal with him!"

Todd, Tracy, and Zoe sat on their ponies and watched as Mr. Fawsley and Jake controlled the pack. Soon, the hounds turned around and streamed back across the fields with Mr. Fawsley and Jake walking along in the middle of them.

"Sounds like Jake is going to get it this time!" Todd said, chuckling.

"Serves him right," Zoe said heatedly. "Maybe he'll think twice before trying to bully anyone else!"

Tracy shrugged. "I wouldn't count on it. Jake's the type to try to get even."

"Just let him try. I'm not scared of him!" Zoe said angrily. *Not while I've got Flame on my side!* she thought.

Chapter
EIGHT

Zoe's mom called a couple of evenings later to say that she had almost finished her book. "I'll be there by the weekend," she told Zoe.

"Great! You can watch me in the riding competition," Zoe said delightedly.

"Your nana told me that you'd made friends with her new next-door neighbors. It sounds like you're having a

great time with the twins and their ponies.
You certainly don't sound like the grumpy
girl I know!" she teased.

"I don't know who you're talking
about!" Zoe said, trying not to laugh. "I'm
glad the writing's going well. See you
soon, Mom. Bye!"

As soon as she put the phone down,
she went to find Flame.

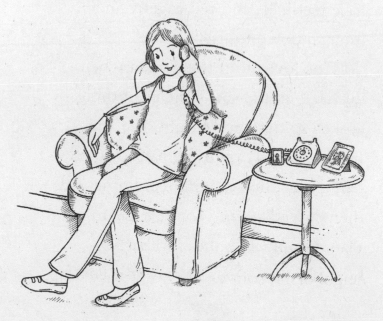

He was curled up on a kitchen chair,
snoozing after finishing his dinner.

Zoe bent down. "Wake up,
sleepyhead," she whispered gently,
stroking his soft fur and breathing in his
sweet kitten smell. "We're going down to
the summer house. I told Todd and Tracy
we'd meet them there."

Flame yawned, showing his sharp
little teeth. He mewed eagerly and
jumped down to follow Zoe.

Zoe loved it in the garden when
dusk fell. In the soft light, everything
looked so fresh and bright. She and
Flame padded down the path that led
past the henhouse and greenhouse and
then curved around to the orchard.
Flame scampered ahead to bat at a
butterfly with one soft paw as it flew up

from a buttercup.

Zoe chuckled at Flame's cute antics. Sometimes she almost forgot that he was really a magnificent lion prince.

There was a bantam hen on the path ahead. It was scratching around, looking for grubs. There was another one, further down the path.

Zoe stopped in surprise. She was sure Nana had put all the bantams in the henhouse for the night. Nana was very careful about that, especially now that Bracken and her cubs were visiting the garden.

Just then, Cocky strutted toward her from the direction of the orchard. His red crest stood up and he ruffled his black wing feathers menacingly.

"What's going on?" Zoe said, looking

around in puzzlement.

Suddenly she noticed that the door to the chicken run was wide open. Someone must have deliberately let out all Nana's bantams!

Zoe heard a faint scrabbling sound. She spun around and saw a dark shape disappearing over the garden wall. It looked like Jake Fawsley. She thought about running to the gate and going after him, but it was more important to get the bantams to safety.

"We have to get them all back inside the henhouse before Bracken discovers them," she said to Flame. "No fox, especially one with cubs, is going to be able to resist an easy meal!"

Zoe dashed forward and tried to grab one of the bantams. Squawking

loudly, it fluttered over a bush. She
lunged at another one, but it avoided
her easily. Cocky gave her a stern look
from his beady red eyes that seemed to
say, "Don't even try it!" Zoe groaned.
"This is hopeless! I'll never catch them
all like this!"

"Do not worry, Zoe. I will help,"
Flame purred.

Big silver sparks glowed in Flame's
calico fur and his whiskers glittered
with electricity, lighting up the dark
garden. Zoe felt her spine tingle as she
wondered excitedly what was about to
happen. Flame pointed a tiny paw at a
garden rake, which was leaning against
the side of the nearby greenhouse. A
big fountain of sparks whooshed out.
There was loud popping sound and the

rake turned into a huge, long-handled fishing net.

"Great!" Zoe said, grabbing it in two hands, realizing what Flame wanted her to do.

Zoe ran to a tree, where a couple of bantams had fluttered up on to a low branch. *Swish!* She scooped them straight into the net, before quickly shutting them away and going in search of the others.

By the time she had swiped up the rest of the hens and shut them away safely, Zoe was bright red and out of breath. "Phew! Everyone's safe—except for Cocky! Now—where is he?"

Flame stood beside her with his ears pricked, looking around helpfully. "I cannot see him."

Suddenly there was a screech as
Cocky launched himself out of an
apple tree, straight at Flame. His strong
clawed feet flexed and he snapped his
beak menacingly.

Flame cringed, completely
surprised by Cocky's attack.

Zoe didn't have the space to swing
the net at the angry bantam cock.
There was no time to think. Dropping

the net, she launched herself at Cocky
and grabbed him in both hands. She
wasn't going to let anything hurt
Flame!

Cocky squealed with rage, thrashing
his feet.

"Oh!" Zoe gasped with pain, as the
razor-sharp claws and spurs raked her
chest. Somehow she managed to keep
hold of Cocky and stagger with him to
the chicken run. She opened the door
with her elbow, threw the cockerel
inside, and latched the door.

Zoe's knees gave way and she sank
on to the grass in shock. The front of
her T-shirt was all ripped. Waves of pain
radiated from the deep scratches.

"You saved my life, Zoe. But you
are hurt!" Flame mewed in concern.

"It doesn't matter. It was worth it," Zoe said bravely, biting her lip. Tears filled her eyes and for one horrible moment, she thought she was going to faint.

Flame's calico fur glittered once more with bright sparks. He leaned forward and very gently breathed out a stream of twinkling rainbow mist.

Warmth seemed to flood over Zoe's chest and she gasped. The scratches tingled sharply for a few seconds and then all of a sudden the pain quickly faded. Zoe put her hands up to her chest. The rips in her T-shirt had mended themselves, too.

She gathered Flame into her arms. "Thanks, Flame. I don't know what I'd do if anything happened to you," she crooned.

Flame gave an extra-loud purr and rubbed his head against her chin. As she stroked him, the last sparks in his fur fizzed against her fingers and went out.

"What are you two doing?" called a cheery voice from behind Zoe.

Todd and Tracy stood there with a bag of leftovers for Bracken and her cubs.

Zoe jumped to her feet with Flame in her arms. "I'll tell you on the way to the summer house!"

Tracy and Todd listened as Zoe told them about the bantams being let out and the shadowy figure she had seen scrambling over the garden wall.

"It had to be Jake Fawsley. The rotten beast!" Tracy burst out.

"I haven't got any proof that it was him," Zoe said reasonably.

"Maybe not. But who else could it have been?" Todd asked.

Zoe shrugged. "I don't know. Anyway, Flame helped me . . . I mean I . . . um, managed to get all the bantams back in, so Jake's plan to get even didn't work."

"I still think we should tell Mr. Fawsley. And I don't care if it means being a tattletale!" Tracy fumed.

"He'd only deny it was him, just like he lied about making Fudge bolt. And it would be his word against ours." Zoe sighed.

The twins looked at each other. They knew Zoe was right.

No one spoke for a while. A few minutes later Bracken and her cubs appeared through the trees and the horrible thought of Jake Fawsley was pushed to the back of everyone's mind.

Chapter
NINE

"I can't believe it's the town fair tomorrow!" Zoe said to her nana at lunchtime the following day.

Joy Swann smiled and handed Zoe a salad. "It's exciting, isn't it? Your mom's arriving first thing, so she can watch you in the competition. And I think I've got a good chance of a getting first prize for my bantams this year."

After lunch, Zoe and Flame went
over to the twins' house. They spent
the afternoon practicing the jumps and
then left the ponies out in the paddock.

Zoe went into the tack room
with Todd and Tracy. They all cleaned
and polished until their arms ached.
Everything had to be gleaming for
tomorrow's show.

Flame curled up on the old wooden

chest, where the horses' brushes and
clean saddle cloths were kept. Zoe
noticed that he kept looking around
anxiously. Once he stood up and stared
into space, the hackles on his back
rising.

Zoe felt a flicker of alarm. What
was wrong with him?

Flame insisted on getting into her
shoulder bag for the short walk back
down the lane to Nana's house. Tucking
himself into a small, tight ball, he
pressed himself into the corner of Zoe's
bag.

She slipped her hand inside to
stroke him. He was trembling all over.
"What's wrong, Flame?" she asked
worriedly.

"I sense my enemies drawing closer.

I may have to leave in a hurry," Flame
whined softly.

"Oh no," Zoe said, feeling her heart
sink.

She had hoped that this day would
never come. Now it looked as if Flame
might have to leave at any moment. She
didn't know how she was going to cope
with losing him.

Zoe felt distraught for the rest of the
evening as Flame was clearly terrified.
She didn't know what to do, except
stroke him reassuringly. That night,
Flame crawled trembling into the back
of Zoe's wardrobe and stayed there. Zoe
lay awake for a long time worrying
about him.

The following morning, however, Zoe was awakened by a little, furry head nudging her cheek. Flame was on her bed. His emerald eyes glowed and he seemed just like his usual self.

"Oh, Flame! You're still here!" Zoe sat up sleepily and gathered him into her arms. She had been almost certain that he'd be gone when she woke up.

"My enemies have passed close by, but they couldn't find me. I think I am safe again for a little while," Flame purred, snuggling up to her.

"I'm so glad," Zoe said with relief. She just hoped his enemies kept on going and never came back.

"Zoe! Are you awake?" a familiar voice called up the stairs.

"Mom!" Zoe leaped out of bed.

She hopped about on one foot as she hurriedly pulled on her jeans and then dragged a brush through her short hair. "Come on, Flame!" she called, racing downstairs.

She threw herself at her mom and gave her an enormous hug.

Zoe's mom smiled. "I've missed you, too! Oh, this must be the kitten I've heard so much about!" She bent down to stroke Flame. "Hello, little one."

Flame gave a little mew of greeting. He rubbed his small furry body against Helen Swann's ankles.

"I've got a feeling he might be coming home with us," Helen said to Zoe.

"Definitely!" Zoe said. She promised herself to keep her fingers and toes crossed that Flame would.

Flame padded after Zoe and her
mom as they went into the kitchen
where Zoe's nana had breakfast ready.
As soon as they had all finished eating,
it was time to get ready for the town
fair.

"Who wants to help me bathe the
chickens?" Joy Swann asked, tying a
bright yellow headscarf over her hair.

Zoe's mom made a face. "That's not
something you get asked every day."

"Come on, Mom, don't be
'chicken'!" Zoe giggled. "I wish I could
help, but I have to go get the ponies
ready with Todd and Tracy." She had
arranged to go to the fair with the
twins and their parents in their cool
horse trailer.

Her mom smiled. "Off you go then,

sweetie. Your nana and I will see you at the show."

Flame trotted at Zoe's heels as she went out the back garden gate and into the lane.

Neither of them noticed the long dark shapes that prowled among the trees in the orchard. "He is very close. We will soon have him!" growled a cold voice.

"Ebony will reward us well," snarled another.

Zoe leaned forward excitedly as the Trapmans' horse trailer turned into the showground. Flame was on her lap, peering out curiously from inside her shoulder bag.

"Wow! It's much bigger than I expected!" She craned her neck, looking at all the white marquee tents, arenas and show pens.

"I've got butterflies in my tummy," Tracy moaned.

"You're lucky. I've got whopping great bats in mine!" Todd said.

Mr. Trapman parked in the lot and Zoe helped the twins get the ponies down the ramp. Flame sat down near

Fudge, watching as Zoe groomed her and tacked up. Eventually all the ponies were ready.

Todd, Tracy, and Zoe changed into matching white shirts, jodhpurs, boots, and hats.

"We still have an hour before the competition. What should we do?" asked Todd.

"We could go and see how my mom and nana are doing with the bantams," Zoe suggested.

She held her bag open, so that Flame could jump in. Shouldering the bag, she walked across the fairground with the twins. As they neared the poultry marquee, a tall boy in riding gear came out.

It was Jake Fawsley.

"Well, if it isn't that nosy kid again!" he sneered at Zoe. "I just saw your nana get first prize. I was surprised she had any bantams left to show. How many did the fox get?"

"So it *was* you who let them all out the other night!" Zoe cried, bunching her fists. "What a terrible thing to do! I should tell your dad what you've been up to!"

Jake sniggered. "I'd like to see you try to prove it!" He walked off, whistling to himself.

Zoe stared after him, fuming.

Todd and Tracy linked arms with her. "Jake's not worth it. Dad says people like him get what they deserve in the end," Todd said.

"That's true," Tracy agreed. "Come

on, let's go congratulate your nana."

"Okay," Zoe said. She put her hand into her bag. As she stroked Flame's soft fur, she felt herself starting to calm down.

Zoe's nana and mom greeted Zoe and the twins with proud smiles. There was a colorful ribbon pinned to Cocky's cage. "Well done, Nana!" Zoe said giving her a big hug. "Isn't it great, Mom?"

"Wonderful! I'm so proud of her," Helen Swann said. "I'm looking forward to seeing you now. How long is it before the competition?"

"About half an hour," Zoe told her.

"I'll see you over there then," her mom said. She pressed some money into Zoe's hand. "Why don't you go and get yourselves an ice cream?"

"Thanks, Mom!" Zoe called over her shoulder, already heading for the ice-cream van.

She, Todd, and Tracy bought double cones. They ate them hungrily as they wandered toward the show-jumping enclosure. Flame stuck his head out of the bag, looking at all the interesting sights. Zoe gave him some ice cream on the end of her finger and giggled as his rough little tongue tickled her.

Zoe suddenly saw a rider on a familiar dark-bay pony who was just beginning his show-jumping round. "Look! It's Jake! Let's go watch him."

They all went and stood by the fence as Jake rode over the jumps. Zoe put her bag on the ground so that Flame could get out and stretch his legs.

Jake's pony cleared the first few jumps easily. But on the next jump, Jake turned his pony sharply as it landed.

"He misjudged that! There isn't room for the pony to get a good run at the jump," Todd said, as Jake approached the water jump. "If he's not careful, the pony will stop before it jumps, and he'll get a refusal."

The bay pony ran toward the fence.
It laid its ears back and faltered. "Go
on!" Jake shouted, slapping it hard on the
rump.

The pony threw down its head and
came to a sudden halt. Jake shot over
its neck and landed head first in the
water. He stood up with water and mud
dripping down his face.

"Oh, bad luck!" Zoe shouted
cheerfully.

The twins were openly laughing.
"It couldn't have happened to a nicer
person!" Tracy said loudly.

Jake glared over at them. He opened
his mouth as if about to say something,
but then seemed to remember all the
people watching. His shoulders sagged
as he squelched around the jump and

picked up his pony's reins. His face was
as red as a tomato.

Still chuckling, Zoe bent down
to pick up her bag. She wondered if
Flame had had anything to do with the
hilarious scene!

"Did you . . . ?" she began to ask
him in a whisper.

But Flame wasn't inside. Zoe looked
all around, but could see no sign of
the tiny calico kitten. Strange. Flame
had never gone off without telling her
where he was going before, especially as
he knew how bad she felt for forgetting
him that one time when she had been
riding Fudge. A dreadful suspicion built
inside her, and her heart thudded.

Zoe hurried toward a nearby
marquee, looking around desperately

for Flame. As she rounded the tent's side, there was a blinding silver flash. Zoe rubbed her eyes and saw Flame standing there, looking magnificent as his true lion self. Silver sparkles glittered in his thick white fur. There was an older gray lion standing next to him.

"I'm sorry. They have come back," Flame's deep voice rumbled sadly.

And then Zoe realized that Flame must leave. However much she adored him, he couldn't stay and be in danger from his enemies.

She ran forward and threw her arms around Flame's muscular neck. "Take care! I'll never forget you!" she said tearfully. She forced herself to stand back. "Go! Quickly! Save yourself!"

Flame nodded. "You have been a good friend. Be well, Zoe."

The old gray lion bowed his head, and there was another bright flash and a shower of sparks that crackled in the grass around Zoe's feet. Flame and the gray lion faded and then disappeared.

Zoe stood there, her heart aching and her throat tight with tears.

"There you are!" called Tracy, running up to her. "Come on. The competition's about to start!"

Zoe rubbed her eyes. She knew that she would never forget the adventure she had shared with the magic kitten. She could never tell anyone about him, but he would be her special secret, forever.

She whirled around to Tracy, feeling excitement starting to push away the sadness. "Wait for me!" she called.

About the Author

Sue Bentley's books for children often include animals or fairies. She lives in Northampton, England, and enjoys reading, going to the movies, and sitting watching the frogs and newts in her garden pond. If she hadn't been a writer, she would probably have been a skydiver or brain surgeon. The main reason she writes is that she can drink cups and cups of tea while she's typing. She has met and owned many cats, and each one has brought a special sort of magic to her life.

Don't miss these Magic Kitten books!

Don't miss these Magic Ponies books!

Don't miss these Magic Puppy books!

Don't miss these Magic Bunny books!

#1 Chocolate Wishes

#2 Vacation Dreams

#3 A Splash of Magic